Blue's Art Day

Published by Advance Publishers, L.C.
www.advance-publishers.com

Written by K. Emily Hutta
Art layout by Niall Harding
Art composition by sheena needham • ess design
Produced by Bumpy Slide Books

ISBN: 1-57973-079-5

Blue's Clues Discovery Series

Hi, there! Blue and I just couldn't stay inside on such a beautiful fall day. We've been out here all morning.

Do you want to see what we're doing? You do? Great!

We're making art with things we find in our backyard—like these leaf rubbings!

I think I'll give my leaf rubbing to my grandma. Who are you going to give yours to, Blue?

Oh! We'll play Blue's Clues to figure out who Blue wants to give her leaf rubbing to! Will you help me? You will? Great!

Thanks, Pail.

I don't think Pail wants to stand on our artwork all day, do you?

I wonder what else we could do to keep it from blowing away.

Maybe we could put something else that's heavy on the papers so they won't blow away. Yeah! But what? A rock? Good thinking! What's that? You see a clue? The spots! Our first clue is spots.

What do you think spots have to do with who Blue wants to give her artwork to? Do you think we need to find two more clues? Yeah, me, too.

Let's paint a rock paperweight to hold our papers down!

Okay. Blue wants to paint the rock to look like that ladybug. Hmmm . . . which rock shape do you think looks the most like a ladybug? Oh. That one. Thanks!

We're done! How does it look? Yeah, I think so, too. I'll just leave it here in the sun to dry.

Oh! You see a clue? A shell! So who could Blue want to give her leaf rubbing to that has spots and a shell? Yeah, I think we need to find our last clue.

Hey, nice picture, Blue. A tree with real leaves. That's so cool!

But why are you sad, Blue? Oh . . . Blue only has three colors, and she wants to make her painting very colorful. Hey! Let's mix colors and make some new ones!

What happens when we mix red and yellow? Right! We get orange. How about blue and yellow? Yeah! Green. And what about red and blue? Purple! We did it! We helped make three new colors for Blue to paint with. Thanks!

Oh, no! It's starting to rain. We'd better take all of our artwork inside. Come on!

Whew! Just in time. What's that? You see a clue! The aquarium. That's our third clue! It's time to go to our . . . Thinking Chair!

Let's see. Our clues are spots, a shell, and an aquarium. So who could Blue want to give her leaf rubbing to? Hmmm. Are you thinking what I'm thinking? Let's ask Blue.

Hey, Blue, do you want to give your leaf rubbing to your pet turtle, Turquoise? You do? We did it! We just figured out Blue's Clues.

It looks like Turquoise loves her picture.
Thanks for helping with Blue's Clues. It sure
was a great way to spend a fall day!

BLUE'S BACKYARD BUG BUDDY

You will need: a rock, acrylic paints, and paintbrushes

1. Look for a rock that's not too small and not too big. Round and oval rocks make great ladybugs. Rinse the rock off and let it dry.

2. Paint the entire rock with red paint. Let it dry.

3. To make the ladybug's face, paint a black semicircle at one end of the rock. To make wings, paint a black line down the middle of the rock. Paint black spots on the wings.

4. Paint eyes and a mouth on the ladybug's face.

5. Make another one for a friend. They make great gifts!